Grandmother Spider Brings the Sun

A Cherokee Story

by Geri Keams *illustrated by* James Bernardin

rising moon

Books for Young Readers from Northland Publishing

To my grandmother, Pansy, my mother, Helen,
and my sister, Patricia, whose stories, wisdom, and teachings
have kept me on the Beauty Way.
—G. K.

To Jeff and Denise, in light of their new marriage.
—J. B.

This book may not be reproduced in whole or in part, by any means
(with the exception of short quotes for the purpose of review),
without permission of the publisher. For information, address
Permissions, Northland Publishing, P.O. Box 1389, Flagstaff, Arizona 86002-1389.

The illustrations in this book were done in
acrylic and color pencil on Crescent Cold Press Illustration Board
The display type was set in Truesdell
The text type was set in Minion
Composed in the United States of America
Manufactured in China

FIRST HARD COVER IMPRESSION, 1995
ISBN 0-87358-597-6

FIRST SOFT COVER IMPRESSION, 1997
ISBN 0-87358-694-8
04 05 06   10   9   8

Library of Congress Cataloging-in-Publication Data
Keams, Geri.
Grandmother Spider brings the sun / by Geri Keams ;
illustrated by James Bernardin.—1st ed.
p.   cm.
Summary: After Possum and Buzzard fail in their attempts to steal a piece of the sun,
Grandmother Spider succeeds in bringing light to the animals on her side of the world.
1. Cherokee Indians—Folklore. 2. Tales—Southern States. [1. Cherokee Indians—Folklore. 2. Indians of North America—
Folklore 3. Folklore—United States. 4. Sun—Folklore.] I. Bernardin, James, ill. II. Title.
E99.C5K35 1995
398.2'089975—dc20   95-2978

A Note from the Author

IN THIS STORY, Grandmother Spider creates a bowl in which fire is carried. To this day, the Cherokee people make clay bowls, which reminds them of Grandmother Spider's remarkable journey.

Just as Grandmother Spider carried her bowl through the long tunnel, Cherokee potters place their bowls of soft clay in a cool, dark place to dry and harden. And just as Grandmother Spider's bowl became stronger as she carried the sun in it, Cherokee potters place their bowls in a hot fire to give them strength.

Grandmother Spider Brings the Sun teaches us to respect and honor Fire, Grandmother Spider, and our four-legged friends, just as the Cherokee do.

A LONG TIME AGO it is said that half the world had the sun, but the other side of the world was very dark. It was so dark that all the animals were always bumping into each other and getting lost.

Wolf lived on this side of the world. He was tired of everybody bumping into him and asking him for directions, for you see, Wolf could see in the nighttime.

Wolf gathered all the animals together in a big cave. He got up in front of them and crossed his arms, and he said, "I am tired of everybody bumping into me and asking me for directions."

"I have an idea," he said. "I think we should go to the other side of the world and ask them for a piece of their sun. I think if we're nice, they'll give us a piece."

Another animal jumped up. This was Coyote, known as the trickster because he lies and cheats and steals.

Coyote said, "No, no, no, no, no! I don't think we should be so nice! If they're so nice, how come they haven't *offered* us a piece of their sun?"

The other animals nodded in agreement.

"I have a better idea," Coyote said. "I think we should sneak over there and just *steal* a piece."

"*Steal* a piece!" said Wolf. "What are you talking about, Coyote?"

"Calm down, calm down, calm down," Coyote said. "We're not going to steal a *big* piece. We'll only take a *little* piece. They'll never even miss it."

And that is what they decided to do.

Then all the animals began asking, "Who is going to go to the other side of the world? How will they get there?" Everybody had an idea, but none seemed quite right.

Then from the back of the room came a small voice. "Hey, I'll go! I'll go!"

Wolf said, "Who is that? Come down here. I can't see you."

Down to the front of the room came a little round animal with chubby cheeks. He was shy and quiet. He stood up in front of all the animals, and as he looked at all those hundreds of eyes looking back at him, he got kind of scared.

He looked out over the crowd of animals and he said in his timid voice, "Hi. M-m-m-my name is Possum. I think I can go to the other side of the world. You see, I've got these long, sharp claws, and I think I can dig a tunnel. And when I go *all* the way to the other side of the world, I'll take a piece of the sun and I'll hide it in my big, bushy tail."

And Wolf said, "Oh, a tunnel! That's the best idea yet!"

So Possum went to the big wall of dirt at the back of the cave, stuck in his sharp claws, and began to dig and dig and dig and dig, faster and faster and faster and faster. Possum disappeared inside the tunnel, and soon he had gone all the way to the other side of the world.

Now, Possum had never seen the sun, so when he popped out on the other side, the light hit his eyes, and he was blinded. His eyes got all squinty and he rubbed them with his dirty fists, saying, "Hey! I can't see!" Well, you know, Possum's eyes have been squinty and ringed with dirt ever since.

Possum struggled over to the sun, took a little piece, and put it inside his big ol' bushy tail. Then he turned around and came running back down the tunnel.

Possum ran faster and faster and faster and faster. Something started to get hot inside his tail, but Possum kept running, faster and faster.

That something got hotter, and Possum kept running faster, and he soon ran into the room where all the animals were waiting. They all saw smoke coming out of his tail, and they screamed, "Possum! Your tail! Your tail!" and threw water on him. *Whoosh! Whoosh! Whoosh!* The light was gone.

When the smoke had cleared, Wolf looked up and said, "Oh, no, Possum! Look at your tail! It's all skinny!"

And you know, Possum's tail has been this way ever since.

Wolf said, "We still don't have any sun. What are we going to do now?"

A loud voice from the back of the room said, "Send me! I'll go!"

Down to the front stormed a large bird with long black feathers all over his body, and a crown of feathers on top of his head. He held his head high and stuck his chest out as he marched importantly past the other animals. You see, this bird was a show-off. He thought he was the most beautiful bird alive.

He stood up in front of all the animal people and he said, "It's me, Big Bad Buzzard. I'll go to the other side of the world and it won't take me long at all, but I wouldn't be so dumb as to hide the light in my tail. I'm gonna hide it in my beautiful crown of feathers."

Buzzard jumped into the tunnel and soared through the darkness, and it didn't take long at all until he came out on the other side.

Buzzard took a little piece of sun, put it inside his crown of feathers, turned around, and soared back down the tunnel faster and faster and faster and faster. As he came down the tunnel, something started to get hot on top of his head.

Buzzard soared faster and faster, and something got hotter and hotter.

Faster he soared, and soon he came into the room where all the animals were waiting. They looked up, and they saw smoke coming from Buzzard's head. "Oh, no! Buzzard! Your head! Your head!" They got water and *Whoosh! Whoosh! Whoosh!* The light went out.

Wolf looked up and said, "Buzzard! You're bald!"

All of Buzzard's feathers crackled and fell down to the ground. Big Bad Buzzard got so shy and quiet that he ran and hid in the back of the room. And you know, Buzzard has been bald ever since, and he still doesn't like anybody looking at him.

Wolf said, "Possum's burned his tail off and now Buzzard's bald, and we still don't have any sun. What are we going to do now?"

A tiny voice from up above said, "Send me, I'll go! Hey, send me, I'll go! I'll go!"

Wolf looked all around, but he couldn't tell where the voice was coming from. "Who is that? Where are you? Come down where I can see you."

Down from the corner of the ceiling squeaked the tiny voice: "Send m e e e e e e e e e e e e ! "

And right there in front of Wolf landed a tiny spider. The spider looked up and Wolf looked down, and Wolf said, "Oh, no! Not you, Grandma! You can't go to the other side of the world. You're too old—and besides that, you're too slow!"

Well, this was Grandmother Spider. She had done many things to help the animals in her long life. She crossed her little arms and said, "I know I'm old. You don't have to tell me I'm old. But I want to help my people one more time. I need a piece of clay about so big, and you'll get me a piece, won't you, son?"

Wolf went and got Grandmother Spider a piece of clay, and she sat in the middle of the room and began to chant. Soon she had worked the clay into a little bowl.

She picked up that beautiful clay bowl and disappeared inside the tunnel. They say it took Grandma Spider a long, long, long, long time to get to the other side of the world.

The Sun Guards were out now. They knew somebody was trying to steal some of their sun, and they stood in a tight circle around it. They weren't going to let anybody through.

The Sun Guards were mean-looking monsters. They had fire coming out of their heads. They had fire coming out of their mouths: *Hisssss!* And they held their weapons, ready for a fight.

But Grandmother Spider was so tiny that they didn't even see her. She sneaked between them, went up to the sun, took a little piece, put it in her clay bowl, and sneaked back past the Sun Guards.

She came back down the tunnel *very* slowly. It took her a long, long, long, long time to get to her side of the world. And as she got closer, something happened. The light inside her bowl began to grow. The little rays stretched out of the bowl.

As she came out of the tunnel into the cave, that ball of light was growing. She could hardly even carry it.

All the animals came running to help Grandmother Spider: blind Possum and bald Buzzard, Wolf and Coyote and Bear and Deer and all the others. But that ball of light just kept getting bigger and bigger and bigger and bigger, and it got so big that the animals had to squeeze it out of the cave, and as it squeezed out into the world it bounced up into the sky: *Boingggg!*

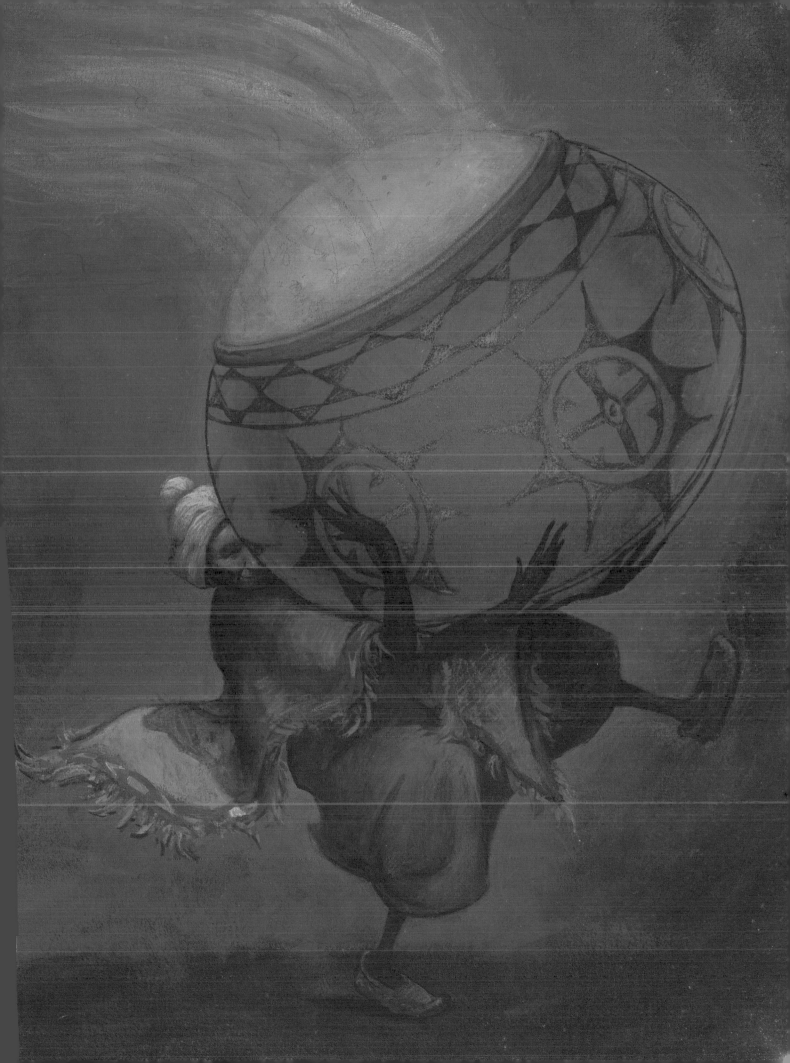

It is said that from that day on, whenever Grandmother Spider would spin her web, the shape of the sun would be at the center. And you see, Grandmother Spider spins her web that way to this very day.

About the Author and Illustrator

Geri Keams was born in the Navajo Nation in Arizona, where she grew up herding sheep, helping her grandmother weave, and listening to the stories of the elders. She is an accomplished actress (best known for her role in the classic Western *The Outlaw Josey Wales,* starring Clint Eastwood), and a professional storyteller recognized for her use of humor. She tells the stories of Native American peoples in order to encourage others to explore Native cultures rather than accept stereotypes. Native legends, creation stories, and chants should be kept alive, Geri says, "for all to hear, to learn, and to honor the earth, our mother."

When **James Bernardin** was a child, his family traveled often. At the beginning of each trip, his parents would give him a new sketchbook to occupy his time. James still does a lot of travel-ing, and his preoccupation with drawing has turned into a successful career. His first book, *Big Men, Big Country,* by Paul R. Walker (Harcourt Brace), earned admiration and praise from a wide audience, and was honored by *American Bookseller* as a "Pick of the Lists." He has since collaborated on two sequel books, *Giants!* and *Little Folks,* with the same author and publisher. James lives in Seattle with his wife, Lisa, and cat, Emily.